WAKE
MAMA!

by **Hope Vestergaard**

illustrations by
Thierry Courtin

Dutton Children's Books • New York

Text copyright © 2003 by Hope Vestergaard
Illustrations copyright © 2003 by Thierry Courtin
All rights reserved.

CIP Data is available.

Published in the United States by
Dutton Children's Books,
a division of Penguin Putnam Books for Young Readers
345 Hudson Street, New York, New York 10014
www.penguinputnam.com

Designed by Beth Herzog
Printed in China
First Edition
ISBN 0-525-47030-1
10 9 8 7 6 5 4 3 2 1

For Carsten—
Keep climbing!

H.V.

Climb your way up Mama Mountain—
Quilt on top and bed below.
Sleepy Mama's not awake yet—
Shhh ... be gentle ... off you go!

Pass her piggies—please don't tickle!
That would surely end this trip!
'Round her knees before she bends them.
See that hill? It's Mama's hip.

Don't stop climbing, you can do it!
Stretch your arms, reach past her side.
Baby, you're just halfway over—
There's no time to horsey-ride!

Fluffy pillows, bumps in blankets—
Warm and toasty from last night.
Here's another—WHOOPS, that's Mother!
Cozy Mama feels just right.

WHOA! She's rolling! Look out, baby!
Now you're safe, she's back to sleep.
Don't get stuck in Mama's nightgown.
Careful as you creep ... creep ... creep.

What's that noise? OH! Mama's snoring!
Humming through her dreams so sweet.
Lay your head down on her tummy.
Feel your Mama's soft heartbeat.

Under elbows—you're so close now!
Sleepy arms give you a squeeze.
Smell her warm skin with your small nose—
Tickly hair makes Mama SNEEZE!

Here's the top of Mama Mountain!
Wake up, Mama! No more rest!
Kiss her, hug her, make her giggle.
Baby wake-ups are the best!